MIN THE FEARLESS

BOOK TWO OF THE DRAGON CHAMPION

MIN THE FEARLESS

BOOK TWO OF THE DRAGON CHAMPION

Becca Lee Gardner

Cover illustration by:
Andrea Quatrini

To Logan,
My cuddly little flurcoon. I love you.

MIN THE FEARLESS

BOOK TWO OF THE DRAGON CHAMPION

PROLOGUE

JURIAN REDGUARD WAS WEARING EVERY piece of his black armor, and he still felt unprotected. Vulnerable.

He'd faced down a dragon—two dragons—while wearing this armor. He'd led the Black Knights into war in this armor.

But now, standing in front of Master Tresach, the most powerful warlock in all of Golshan, he wished he had more armor.

Warlock Tresach stood by a window, and he wore no armor at all. His black hair fell down his back, and he was taller than any soldier Jurian had seen. The warlock was strong. His muscles showed beneath his long, dark blue robe, and Jurian was very sure Master Tresach could kill him without any magic at all.

The air was colder around the warlock. And quieter.

Animals didn't make sounds around him. Not birds. Not hunting dogs. Cats wouldn't be in the same room as him. Even mice chose other chambers in the castle to scavenge for scraps.

"You are sure the second dragon wore a ring around its neck?" Tresach asked. He didn't speak loudly, but in the silence that seemed to follow him, his words commanded the room.

Jurian wanted to shiver, but he clenched his jaw and kept himself standing straight. "Yes, Master Tresach."

Tresach turned and Jurian flinched.

Today the warlock had golden eyes. Sometimes they glowed blue, and sometimes they were golden. But each time they turned on Jurian, he wished the warlock would look away.

"My granddaughter was with this dragon?" Tresach asked.

"It saved her," Jurian said, his voice squeaking a little. "And it transformed from a small dragon to a large. And back again. They were with another dragon. One they called Kerr."

Tresach flexed his hand, and Jurian wanted to flee the room. It felt like the warlock might transform his anger into a magical spell at any moment and fling it at Jurian.

Instead, Tresach clenched his jaw tight. "Orion, what mischief have you conjured?" he muttered.

Jurian shivered. He'd been in battles with the enormous, white dragon known as Orion. The knights called him the Friendless Fiend because when Orion joined the battle, every human was in peril, no matter which army they fought for.

"Have you tracked my granddaughter since the battle?" Tresach asked.

"Yes," Jurian replied. "They went east. To Mirror

Lakes."

Tresach's mood seemed to shift in an instant. Violence shifting to glee. "They're gathering the Elemental Dragons. They mean to make war."

Tresach laughed, and the sound made the room feel like winter. Jurian took two steps backward toward the door before he regained control and forced himself to stay and listen to the horrible sound. Tresach laughing was scarier than him yelling.

"Bring Warlock Rallen in," Tresach said when he'd finished with the terrible laughter. "If they would do war against me, it will begin in Yawen."

Jurian bowed and hurried out of the room.

He obeyed Tresach's orders and then retreated to his room in the castle, where he sat beside the fire for hours but could not get warm.

1

Min beat her wings hard against the cold, morning air, but she still couldn't catch Kerr.

The Earth Dragon hurtled through the sky, spinning through the clouds and bursting them into tiny, white, fluffy pieces.

Those bits of white fluff trailed behind the massive dragon and littered the air around Min. She ducked and turned, dodging the first few tufts of clouds until one clobbered her in the face. In an instant all she could see was white, and droplets of water coated her nose and mouth. The water tasted like rain and sunshine.

Shaking her head, Min broke free of the cloud and looked up at the Earth Dragon. He'd flown even higher than before, weaving and dancing with the clouds as they changed colors with the sunrise. At first, the clouds had been pale grays and whites, but now they exploded with color: deep purples and lake blues all hemmed with a red almost as vibrant as Min's own scales.

Kerr burst through the colorful air. His own greens and browns looked strange in the sky, like a mountain soaring in the wind.

Min's wings felt heavy, and something loud inside her said she should head back to the ground right now. She looked down. They'd flown a long way from their camp below. Abigail was barely a speck walking along the edges of the lake. If something happened to Min's wings now, she wouldn't survive the fall.

"You're scared of falling, Little One."

Min remembered the time the murada lizard hit her with poison. She'd spun helplessly in the air. Her wing had stopped working and she'd fallen. Down, down, down. Abigail had caught her and saved her from crashing into the rocks.

If she fell now, would Abigail be able to catch her again?

Min's vision blurred and her wings didn't flap quite right. Air gushed around her. She tried to beat her wings, but she was spinning in all directions. Falling again! She was falling again!

She chirped a terrified sound. Then something as solid and warm as the earth itself—green and gold and wider than twenty Mins—appeared beneath her.

Kerr. Kerr had flown beneath Min, and he caught her.

She panted, and her claws clung to the large dragon's scales as he navigated the air with ease. Silent and calm.

"Falling is part of flying, Little One," Kerr said.

Min wanted to argue with the Earth Dragon, but she was still trying to catch her breath.

Kerr flew in silence for a few minutes. When Min had settled down a little more, he asked, "Does the air still call to you?"

Min wanted to say no. She wanted to tell Kerr that

Orion's ring on her neck was calling her to the Water Dragon or Fire Dragon or Ice Dragon. Even the Shadow Dragon!

But that would be a lie.

Even though flying terrified Min, the air still called to her. Min gulped and tried to make her small voice sound mighty, "It does. I must save the Air Elemental Dragon."

2

MIN SPENT THE REST OF THE DAY ON THE BEACH. Away from camp. Away from Kerr and Abigail. And very, very close to a sly crab. The thing was the size of her foot. It had specks of orange and black on its back and had one bright blue claw.

She stalked close to the crab, easing her feet into the sand and using each muscle as slowly as she could.

Her toe scratched a rock, and the crab heard her.

It leapt into action and burrowed down into the sand, disappearing in the blink of an eye.

Min lowered her belly down to the ground, held her wings tight against her body, and waited. Sure enough, the crab pushed out of the sand a few feet away. Its long eyes popped out of the sand first, then its speckled body, and finally its bright blue claw.

Min began her slow approach once more. She avoided every rock and pebble around her.

She crept closer and closer to the crab. Three more careful steps and she'd be able to snap up the crab like a giant bug and crunch it between her tiny, sharp teeth.

Then Abigail stomped down the beach with her heavy, clumsy human feet. Each footstep might as well have been thunder.

The crab spun around, pinched its blue claw at Min, and burrowed again.

Min blew a stream of fire at the sand where the crab had just been, then curled up there to wait.

"I've made food," Abigail said in Drakon. Her pronunciation was getting better every day. Kerr had helped with that. "You don't need to eat crabs."

"I am not eating crabs. I am hunting crabs," Min said.

Abigail set a linen sack and her notebook on the sand. Min hadn't seen the human go anywhere for weeks without her notebook. She spent hours and hours every night talking with Kerr and scribbling in her notebook until the fire faded to embers. Min had watched her do it for the first few nights, marveling at how strange human words looked on the page. Then Min had opted to sleep through the whispered discussions, enjoying the comforting rumble of another dragon's voice.

"Hunting?" Abigail asked.

"Yes."

Abigail folded her legs beneath her. Her long, blue tunic dress was stained with berry juice, and twigs were stuck in her braided, black hair. "You're upset."

"No," Min said. "I am a hunter."

Abigail smiled. "You can be an upset hunter."

The crab's eyes popped out of the sand and looked around. Min lifted her chin and stared at the crab. It didn't seem to notice her, so she rose up onto her feet, crouching low.

Then Min pounced.

The crab darted back into the ground, burrowing into the sand faster than Min's claws could dig. She churned up piles and piles of sand. But the crab was gone.

When she finally stopped digging, Min spat fire where she'd last seen the crab. And then she shot a few more spits of flame where she guessed the crab might be now.

"Hunters don't get upset, eh?"

Min glared at Abigail. "Not upset. Striking fear into my prey."

Abigail pulled a twig from her hair and flicked it away. "Kerr said you still feel pulled to fly. The ring still wants you to save the Air Dragon."

Min's tail flicked. She felt the itch to fly right now. To dance among the clouds. But as soon as she thought about being in the air, she remembered the sensation of falling, and that blissful impulse went stale and dry like a leaf falling from a tree in autumn.

"Sora is the name of the Air Elemental Dragon. She lives in a city in the clouds."

Min snapped her teeth at the sand and the crab somewhere safe beneath it. "You've told me all this before."

Abigail smiled. Min flicked her tail faster. Harder. She remembered when she first saw the human smile. She'd thought it was a threat then. Now it was just annoying. Smug.

"We know it's not easy to be the Dragon Champion," Abigail said. "But we believe in you. You'll make it to the sky city. You'll save Sora."

The crab popped out of the sand mere inches from Min's claws. Instead of burrowing farther away from Min, it had drawn closer.

Min looked up at Abigail.

Abigail shook her head.

But the human couldn't tell her what to do. Min was a dragon! And a hunter!

She lunged at the crab and caught it between her front claws. She held it there, tight enough that it couldn't escape, but soft enough that no injury came to it—yet.

The crab scuttled about within its cage and pinched at Min's red scales with its bright blue claw. But it was no use.

Min's throat fire grew warmer and warmer. She could roast this little bit of prey. She'd won, after all. And she was a dragon—a hunter.

The crab stopped fighting and stayed very still inside its cage. Min could imagine its fear. Min must be enormous to the little crab, and she'd stalked it across the beach, never giving up, until she now had it powerless in her grip.

She'd made it afraid.

She'd become a hunter because she was afraid to fly.

With a sigh, Min let the crab go. It scurried out of her claws and dug a quick escape into the sand.

"That was good of you, Min," Abigail said.

"I'm still a hunter," Min said.

Abigail smiled again. "Of course you are. Let's go get this hunter some dinner, eh? It's waiting for you at camp."

Min and Abigail walked back to camp. The human took tiny step after tiny step to walk side-by-side with Min. She clutched the bag and book to her chest.

"Little One," Kerr rumbled. His words traveled through the ground and were sharp and urgent. "Come to me. Now!"

3

FOR A MOMENT, Min ran toward Kerr but couldn't see any sign of him. Their camp was hemmed in with boulders the sizes of Kerr's arms or head or body.

Then several of the stones moved, lifting up into the air, and Min made out Kerr's head, neck, body and tail. He looked like a mountain with green and gold eyes that stared up at the sky.

She leapt onto the massive dragon's claw and climbed a familiar path up Kerr's forearm and shoulder and neck until she was atop the other dragon's head. She halted and looked about the rocky shore.

Their camp was tucked between a stone cliff and a lake shore. Atop the cliff, golden grasses and tiny, blue flowers grew and swayed in the breeze. Above the sand and rocks and cliffs and grasses stretched a sky painted in a sunset of blues and purples.

And there, in the clouds, were speckles of black.

At first, they looked like they could have been black

leaves caught up in the wind, swirling about in the sunset. But the specks didn't move with the wind. And they were larger than leaves. Much, much larger.

"There's something there," Min said.

"Do you feel them?" Kerr asked.

Min made a face. "Feel what?"

Kerr raised his head higher as though he were looking toward the black specks, but his eyes were closed. "Feel."

Min closed her eyes. She did feel things. She felt irritated that Kerr was asking her to feel. She felt hungry. And she felt . . . her heart beating fast . . . her throat fire growing hot. "There's danger," Min said.

"Yes," Kerr said. "That is what I feel too."

"What are they?" Min asked.

"Dorcha!" Abigail blurted out. The human had run after Min and was panting beside Kerr's front legs.

"Dorcha?" Min asked.

"Are you sure?" Kerr said with a rumble.

Abigail, still breathing hard, pointed to a page in her notebook. "Yes."

Kerr stood, and Min had to duck low to stay on the Earth Dragon's head.

"We need a place to hide," Kerr said.

"What is a dorcha?" Min asked.

"I found a cave," Abigail said. "It was near the berry patch."

"What is a dorcha!" Min yelled more than asked.

Kerr ignored Min. "Will the cave fit you and Min?"

Abigail snapped her notebook shut. "Yes!"

"What are the dorcha!" Min roared, and she shot a burst of flame at Kerr's horns.

"Not now, Little One!" Kerr bellowed the words, louder and more forceful than Min had ever heard him speak.

Min swallowed her throat fire. It still burned and sloshed around in her belly. Hot and uncomfortable. She wanted to let it out along with more of her questions. She wanted Abigail and Kerr to share their knowledge. Instead, she clung to Kerr's head as he ran down the length of the beach, past a patch of thorny berry bushes, and to a dark cave.

The black specks—whatever the dorcha were—grew larger and larger by the second. What had first looked like leaves were now the size of Kerr's paw and still a ways off.

"They feel your magic," Abigail said to Kerr.

Kerr stared up at the sky. "They'll feel the ring's magic clearer than my own."

Min glided down from Kerr's back. Abigail rushed into the dark cave. Kerr settled his body nearest the rocks, crouching down until his scales blended with the stone. Min hesitated outside the cave.

Kerr turned one golden eye on Min and grumbled a sound that contained a hundred words.

Min got the message. She quietly hurried inside the darkness of the cave but stopped where she could still see the sky and the clouds and Kerr.

She waited and watched. The dorcha, flapping big, leathery wings, circled downward and landed on the beach. They had brown skin and short, bristly hair all over their bodies. They were bats. Giant bats. They crawled about the sand on their bellies, using the hooks on the ends of their wings to pull themselves this way and that.

Twelve dorcha sniffed around on the sand with wet snuffling sounds. Half of them moved toward the camp where the fire still burned. And the other half wriggled across the ground toward the cave and the hiding dragons.

Abigail's footsteps were as loud and clumsy as ever as she moved closer to Min and knelt beside her.

The dorcha heard the human's movement and hurried toward the sound. The creatures whined a hungry sort of whine.

"We have to go deeper in the cave," Abigail whispered. "We can't let them find you."

"Why me?"

"Dorcha are attracted to magic," she said in a whisper. "They'll attack you."

"I'm not leaving Kerr."

Abigail let out a long breath. "Kerr's magic is a whisper. It's natural to the world. Like a river. The ring on your neck? It's a red moon. It used to be natural, but it's been twisted by Warlock magic. And the dorcha hate Warlock magic."

"Orion the dragon made this ring."

"With my grandfather the warlock. Trust me, Min. The dorcha will come for you first."

"I'm not going to leave Kerr," Min growled. "We can fight them. Together."

A rumble emanated from where Kerr lay. But this time Kerr wasn't speaking a warning to Min. He was moving the earth itself.

Rocks broke free from the cave entrance and tumbled down around them. Min and Abigail fell backward just before the stones piled up in front of them, blocking the entrance.

On the other side of the rock barrier, the dorcha squealed.

"Kerr!" Min roared. "Kerr!"

4

MIN PRESSED HER HEAD AGAINST the rocks separating
her from Kerr, the dorcha, and the beach beyond. She'd
heard the first strange squeal from the dorcha, but not a
sound after.

Did that mean that the dorcha had hurt Kerr? Had
they taken him away? Could they do either of those
things? Kerr was one of the Elemental Dragons, after all.
Surely he could handle himself.

But he had ordered Min into the cave. He'd been
cautious of the dorcha. Wary.

Min strained to hear even a murmur of sound, and
long minutes stretched by. Abigail fumbled around in the
dark to grab Min. Min spat flames near the human's
hands, and she didn't try again.

Min's heart slapped around her ribcage, and she
imagined every awful thing that could happen to Kerr.
Her throat fire grew hotter and hotter. She pulled her
head away from the rock and aimed a jet of her fiercest

flame at it. The stone glowed with the heat and lit up the cave for a few seconds.

But when the light and heat were gone, the rocks remained. And Min was left with her feelings.

She closed her eyes and felt her panic and fear and anger—like thorns in her mind. But she moved beyond them until she felt a cool, calm presence she recognized.

Kerr.

Kerr was alive. He was still just outside the rock wall he'd created between them. She felt him there. She couldn't see him or smell him, but she knew he was there. She just knew.

She felt the dorcha too. They were like fire ants, biting and burning across her thoughts.

But there was something else. Someone else.

Min felt another dragon.

The dragon was far away and above them. She was bright and playful and sad and quiet all at once.

"I feel her," Min said.

"Did you find something?" Abigail asked. Then she tripped over a rock and crashed into the dirt. She got a lot of bruises trying to see in the dark like a dragon. Silly human.

Min felt the dorcha leave. Then the rocks blocking the entrance began to shift and move. Light trickled into the cave, and a shadow crossed into the light.

"They're gone," Kerr said.

"Did they attack you?" Abigail asked.

"No," Kerr said. "I kept myself hidden."

"Why do they hate Warlock magic?" Abigail asked.

"They have every reason to despise Warlock magic," Kerr said. "They have never seen it used for good."

Kerr leaned close to Min and touched his nose to her back. "Are you okay, Little One?"

Min looked up at Kerr for the first time since he'd opened the cave. "I felt her," she said. "I felt Sora."

5

MIN DIDN'T SLEEP MUCH THAT NIGHT. She spent the hours thinking about when she'd found Kerr. He'd almost forgotten he was a dragon. He'd thought he was just a mindless, unfeeling stone rather than the majestic creature who could wield it.

Was Sora just as bad? What if Min was too late, and Sora forgot that she was a dragon?

She couldn't let that happen.

When the morning light came, and the sunrise threw pink and gold and orange banners out across the sky, Min knew what she needed to do.

She crawled down from her rock and marched right up to Kerr's face. The Earth Dragon breathed out big, billowing breaths that made puffs of little brown clouds in the dirt.

Min settled herself right in front of Kerr's closed eye and said, "I am going to fly to the city of Yawen. Today. Now."

Kerr opened his huge, golden eye and let out a long, tired breath. "Breakfast first, Little One?"

"No," Min said. "Sora needs me now."

Kerr smiled and raised his head from the ground. He stretched his back up and his wings out, shaking the sleep and dirt from his body. "Then it will be a small breakfast."

Abigail shot to her feet. Her hair stuck up at odd angles. It looked like she'd been struck by lightning while she'd slept. Or had wrestled a bear.

"What's wrong? Where are you going? Who's coming?" Abigail muttered, still half asleep.

"I'm going to Yawen," Min said. "I'm going to save Sora."

Abigail's eyes opened all the way. "When?"

"Now," Min pronounced. Her wings itched to beat up into the sky, but fear fluttered in her heart too.

"Will the dorcha be a problem?" Abigail asked, her notebook suddenly in her hand as she flipped through the pages. Had she slept with the notebook too? Or did it just appear in her hands whenever she had questions.

"The dorcha are most active at dawn and dusk," Kerr said. "And they'll stay close. They caught the scent of Min's ring last night. I was able to hide most of it with the avalanche. But they'll return. They do not forget a smell."

"So, we're leaving in the afternoon," Abigail said, her voice a little calmer.

"We're leaving now," Min said.

"Kerr just told us that the dorcha will be most likely to find you in the morning. We should leave lat—"

Min didn't let Abigail finish. "Sora needs me. We leave now."

Abigail gave Kerr a shrug. The big dragon rumbled a little laugh.

"You want to convince Min to wait, even a few minutes?" Kerr asked.

"I'd rather dance with the dorcha," Abigail replied, then laughed a little herself. "I'll see what we can eat fast."

6

KERR INSISTED THAT THEY EAT BREAKFAST. Even a small one.

Min ate three butterflies. The yellow tasted the best. Sweet and crunchy. The red one was spicy. And the blue and black one tasted like mushrooms.

She didn't like mushrooms.

It wasn't a full meal, but it was enough to stop her stomach from making loud grumbling sounds. She still had quieter gurgles and groans, but Min could live with that.

She was much too nervous to have a full stomach anyway.

Kerr could help her get close to the city of Yawen, high up in the clouds, but he couldn't land there. Earth and Air magic didn't agree with each other. If Kerr landed in Yawen, he could accidentally make the whole city fall out of the sky just by being too close. It wasn't a risk they could take.

Kerr would fly with Min as close as he could, and she would have to go the last bit on her own.

"You won't be able to see Yawen until you get right up to it," Abigail said, reading from her notebook. "It will look like a rainbow. Or so I've read."

Min stretched her wings in and out nervously. "And you won't be there to help me."

"I'll come as soon as I can," Abigail said, with a sad smile. "There are sky trains to Yawen. I'm so excited to ride one! They are powered by Sora's magic, and they transport people from the cities on the ground all the way to Yawen in the sky. But only certain cities have sky train stations, and I'll have to get to one first. It will take one day. Maybe two."

Min shook her head. "One or two days?"

"Hopefully one," Abigail said. "But with the dorcha hunting, I'll have to walk. Well, both of us will walk. As soon as Kerr gets back from taking you as high as he can, I guess."

"The warlock in Yawen isn't there. At least not now," Abigail said. "Last time we were near a city, I heard the merchants talking. Warlock Rallen has been called away. You might be able to save Sora before the warlock even returns to the city."

Min's chest felt tight, and that panic came again. She'd be alone in Yawen. No Kerr. No Abigail. Just Min sneaking about while the warlock was supposed to be gone. But if they wanted to free Sora, this was the best time to do it.

Kerr strode up beside Min. His footsteps were heavy, but the ground seemed to sing under him. Nothing like the chaotic tremors that Abigail caused any time she moved.

"You will get to Yawen, Little One," Kerr rumbled.

"And you will free Sora."

Min nodded. She glanced at the wonderfully safe ground around her, then felt out for Sora somewhere above them. She still felt the other dragon, like a song only her heart could hear.

She took a running start, hurtled to the top of a rock, and leapt into the air.

She beat her wings hard and, in a moment, was already dozens of feet above Abigail's head. Relishing the sun and the wind, Min fought the fear as it started bubbling up through her chest.

With a mighty leap and a gush of air, Kerr launched from the ground to join Min in the sky.

Min led the way, following that song in her heart that told her where Sora was. And Kerr kept pace with Min, his head moving back and forth—keeping guard.

Min focused on each beat of her wings and on the joyful sensations that rushed through her. She tried not to look at how far away the ground was below her.

And she worked to convince herself that Kerr would be with her most of the way to Yawen.

Just when Min's heart began to settle and her wings beat to a steady rhythm, she felt that spike of fear return.

"The dorcha!" Kerr rumbled. "They're back!"

7

THE DORCHA RUSHED AT THEM from behind a cloud and surrounded Min and Kerr in a moment. They dove in from above with claws that tried to grab Min and the ring on her neck.

Kerr roared and snapped his massive jaws at the creatures. They dodged the strikes and pivoted toward Min again.

She beat her wings more frantically than ever. She no longer felt the joy of flying. Instead, she felt a cold fear like a weight in her belly, threatening to slow her down. To make her easier for the dorcha to get. To send her plummeting to the ground.

"Fight!" Kerr bellowed.

Min winged harder, and she released throat fire at the next set of claws that swiped at her.

It worked. The claws retreated with a screeching sound.

"Stay at my belly," Kerr yelled in the wind. "And

FIGHT!"

Kerr rolled to the left. His huge wings buffeted and pushed Min. She fought the wind Kerr created and flapped her tiny wings to stay beneath him, blowing out bursts of fire at anything that wasn't Kerr.

Kerr aimed them upward. Min fought to keep pace with the larger dragon. The dorcha screeched all around them.

"You have to keep going," Kerr rumbled low in his throat. Min was near the dragon's chest, so she caught the words. "Yawen is ahead. I can feel Sora close."

"The dorcha will get me," Min yelled into the wind. Even before the dorcha ambushed them, she'd been scared to make the last bit of the journey alone. Now she would have to find Yawen, not fall to the ground, *and* keep out of the dorcha's claws.

"I'll fight as many as I can," Kerr said. "Go high and fast, Little One."

Min wanted to tell Kerr how afraid she was. But this was for Sora. And Min was more than just a dragon—she was the Dragon Champion.

Kerr pitched to the left and reversed his direction to fly right at the group of dorcha. Min kept flying higher and higher. She fought the urge to look back as Kerr roared and the dorcha screeched.

She passed through a puff of white clouds. Then another.

Her wings were more tired than they'd ever been. She still had more to go. How much more? She had no idea.

She could try for hours and not find Yawen. Then she'd fall. She'd fall, and Kerr wouldn't be ready to catch her. He'd be fighting the dorcha. She'd fall, and Abigail wouldn't be there to stop her from hitting the rocks. . . .

A glimmer of light pulled Min a little higher. Purples

and reds and oranges, yellows and greens and blues.

A rainbow.

Min beat her heavy wings again and again. She was slowly getting closer and closer to the spectacular light strung between two white clouds.

A screech blared in Min's ears, and she ducked into a turn. Dorcha claws missed Min's head by inches. She spat fire at the thing and kept flying higher. She pushed herself harder and flew faster than she'd ever flown before. She had to reach Yawen before the dorcha snatched her up.

The rainbow was closer now. The air felt warmer, wetter, and she blinked the moisture from her eyes. The dorcha didn't scream again, but Min didn't look back to see if it was following. She just flapped and flapped and flapped until she burst into the rainbow, and the colors exploded all around her.

8

As soon as Min burst through the rainbow of colors, she lost control of her tired wings, and tumbled downward. Everything was a blur and she began to fall.

For a moment she wondered if she'd fall all the way back down to the ground. Or if she'd just fall far enough for the Dorcha to get at her.

As soon as Min burst through the rainbow of colors, she lost control of her tired wings and tumbled downward. Everything was a blur.

For a moment she wondered if she'd fall all the way back down to the ground. Or maybe she'd fall just far enough for the dorcha to get at her.

But she only fell a couple of feet and landed on a street made of silver stones. Houses lined the street on both sides. Some of their walls were plain white, while others were mixtures of bright orange and purple and reds that seemed to change and shift while Min watched.

Beyond the street and houses rose a magnificent tower. It looked round, like it had been built by piling clouds on top of each other until the building was the highest in the city.

Min had made it to Yawen.

In a flash of purple, something collided into Min and pinned her down. Min fought back, but then she had a strange feeling and stopped.

A strange creature with bright purple fur stood atop Min's chest. It had triangular ears, a round body, four legs, and a purple-striped fluffy tail, which flicked back and forth. Its face had three white stripes, all of which pointed to its big, black nose.

Min should have attacked this creature. She should have blown fire at it and bit at it. But something deep inside her didn't ever want to hurt it, so she stayed very still. And the creature pressed that black nose close to Min and sniffed and snuffed her up and down, breathing in all of Min's smells in a few seconds. It was twice as big as Min, but it held her pinned down with gentle paws, and it stared at her with round, curious, turquoise eyes.

"Get off," Min said. "Please."

The creature cocked its head. And it moved off of Min.

Min blinked. The creature had just understood Drakon!

Not even the crows in Min's old forest had understood Drakon. They were clever birds and had picked up a few words. But mostly Min had communicated with her teeth and fire while they talked back with their constant, mocking laughter.

How did this creature know Drakon?

"Get out of here ya' bushy-tailed menace!" A new voice shouted in Humanish. The creature hissed, showing its bright white teeth, and then it scampered away and soared into the sky, twirling and flying without any wings at all.

"Master Rallen would do well to exterminate those things," the voice said. Min had been learning her Humanish with Kerr and Abigail, so she understood the words the old man spoke. He wore a big circle hat and a blue vest. His wrinkly, thin arms held a basket of strange-looking roots. He shook a fist at the sky. "Flurcoons are nothing but pests!"

Immediately Min wanted to scurry away. She'd only interacted with three humans, and two of the three had tried to kill her. The other one was Abigail.

Min rolled to her feet, but her legs wobbled beneath her, and her wings lay limp on the ground. She was tired. More tired than she'd ever been before. She couldn't fly away from the human. She couldn't even run. She'd be lucky to stand for a moment or two.

So she coiled her legs beneath her body, folded her wings in tight to herself, and showed her teeth at the human.

The human paused and looked Min up and down. "You're a strange little bird, ain't you?"

Min wanted to roar at the man. She was not a bird!

But she realized that announcing she was a dragon may not be wise. So she kept the roar in her belly and snapped her tiny, white teeth at the man's hand instead.

"I won't do ya any harm," he said with a little chuckle. "Are you hurt?"

He tried to touch her wing, and she bit at his finger. Her teeth didn't touch the human's skin, but she got close enough to smell it. And she was very, very glad she didn't have to bite the human. Humans must taste awful! The smell was bad enough!

"Okay. Okay. I won't touch you." He rifled about in his basket and pulled out a strange-looking plant with bright blue flowers, and leaves with black stripes down them. "Eat the flowers first. Save the leaves for when you have the stomach for it. They'll give you back your strength, but they'll also make you vomit, if you're not careful."

Min let the man put the offering down on the ground beside her without attacking his hand again.

He lingered there for a moment. And Min eyed the bit of tan skin showing over his slippered foot. She'd attack there if he tried to take her.

"Welcome to Yawen, you strange little thing. Mind the rivers, they pour out into the sky. And don't turn your back on the flurcoons. You're lucky they didn't bite you the first time!"

Min snapped her tiny teeth, and the man chuckled again. Then he straightened and shuffled away. He crossed a bridge over water that swirled with a rainbow of colors and then continued on into the city.

Min wrapped her claws around the odd root vegetable and stared up at the city. Relieved and scared at the same time.

9

MIN ATE THE BLUE FLOWERS IMMEDIATELY.

She'd only had the butterflies to eat for breakfast—and no dinner before that. The flight to the city of Yawen had left her dizzy with hunger and fatigue. So she ate the blue flowers, and they were delicious. They tasted like the air after a good rain, fresh and sweet and hopeful.

With the flowers in her belly, Min tried the leaves of the plant.

Those tasted like humans. Or mushrooms. Or human mushrooms. YUCK!

She almost barfed the leaf out. But she kept it down and swallowed that bitter, dirty, ugly taste into her belly.

She left the rest of the plant on the side of the road for someone braver or more desperate than her to eat.

As soon as she turned her back on the weird plant, one of the flying, purple, furry things came diving down to grab it. Min leapt back, wings out wide and teeth bared, but the creature didn't leap upon her again.

It plucked up the food and held it in its paws.

What had the old man called this thing again?

A flurcoon.

The flurcoon looked a little sad as it studied the food, like it desperately wanted to eat it but couldn't for some reason. Then the creature sank into the ground, dissolving into whatever cloudy, solid substance that made the city.

The strange vegetable sat on the street, right where the flurcoon had been.

Min stared at the spot for a long breath. Was that normal? Did the animals that lived on Yawen all melt into clouds?

These weren't even the biggest of Min's questions. The biggest question was where she should go next. She needed to find Sora before Warlock Rallen returned to Yawen. But where should she look first?

Warlock Loatra had hidden Kerr in the depths of the city. Would Sora be the same?

Abigail and her notebook would know the answers to all of these big questions—or at least know how to begin to answer them. But Abigail was somewhere on the land, miles and miles below Yawen. And there was no one here to ask for help.

Just then two purple, fuzzy ears popped out of the ground. They looked like they were tiny, purple mountains jutting out of the stone. The ears rose higher, and now Min could see the big turquoise eyes, the three white stripes on either side of its face, and that big, wet, black nose.

The flurcoon was back. It peeked its head out of the ground, with its body still submerged. It looked like a frog watching her from a pond. But the pond was a stone street in a city that floated in the sky.

At first, Min wanted to spit fire at the thing. She didn't need any distractions right now! What she needed was to find Sora.

But there was something about the flurcoon. It felt familiar, like she'd met it before.

Min swallowed the throat heat. "I need help," she said. "I need to find Sora."

The flurcoon pushed two of its paws up onto the street and rested its furry purple head on them.

"Do you know where she is?"

The flurcoon chittered and whined at Min.

"Is that a yes?"

The flurcoon launched into the sky, bending and twisting its cloud-like tail as it rolled around the air like an otter in the water.

"Guess not," Min said, and she started toward the bridge where she'd seen the old human go.

A blur of purple flashed in front of Min, and she had to dig her claws into the stone street to keep from running into the flurcoon.

The chittering flurcoon circled Min.

Min's throat fire grew hot, and she didn't swallow it down this time. "Leave me alone. I need to find Sora."

Min took a step toward the bridge, and the flurcoon dove right in front of Min, spinning and disappearing into the street.

Min took another step, and the flurcoon exploded out of the street right in front of her and then up into the sky. It turned quickly to face Min and began its high-pitched squeaks and chatter again.

"You don't want me to go on the bridge?" Min asked.

The flurcoon quieted in an instant and nodded its head.

"Where should I go then?" Min asked. "I have to find

Becca Lee Gardner

Sora."

The flurcoon flew straight up a few feet and waited for Min. Then flew straight up and waited again.

"You want me to follow you," Min said.

The flurcoon nodded.

Min sighed. "More flying. Great."

10

MIN CROUCHED LOW, dug her claws into the stone, pushed up into the sky, and flapped her red wings slow and hard. The strange vegetable root had done its job, and Min's body didn't hurt as much. With each beat of her wings, flying became easier.

The flurcoon dove and spun in the sky. Min had never seen anything like it. Spinning and turning, dipping and dancing, the purple, furry creature seemed to be made of the cloud itself, and it cut through the air as easily as Kerr did stone.

Min found herself eager to catch up to the flurcoon. She was even more eager to mimic the creature's movements—to feel its joy.

As she raced after the creature, Min let herself spin a little to the left. She told herself she was just following the flurcoon, but that wasn't completely true. She felt the stirring of joy in her chest, and spinning in the air, even once, seemed to unlock that happiness like a door creaking open little by little to let in the daylight.

Before she realized it, a dozen flurcoons had joined the first. They surrounded Min and danced with her in the sky. Urging her onward. Teaching her how to spin and roll in the air. Min followed as best she could, but her wings got in the way as she tried to turn as fast as the flurcoons.

After what seemed like hours in the sky, the flurcoons descended to land in a meadow of tall grass the color of the sun. Min followed the flurcoons. When she got to the ground, the flurcoons were already running to form a large circle in the grass. More and more flurcoons joined the ones that had teased Min on the way here. Soon, the circle of flurcoons was big enough that Kerr could have landed in the middle, rolled over, and taken a nap without ever getting close to knocking over a flurcoon.

Min stood slightly back from the gathering. The flurcoons acted strange, but Min kept getting the sensation that she'd met these creatures before. They hadn't been in her old forest. And they hadn't been in Avani with Kerr. So where would she have met them?

The Flurcoons howled in unison, and the sound was sad. Like they were calling for something—or someone— they'd lost.

"Sora," Min said. Finally, she understood. She'd asked the flurcoons to show her where Sora was. Instead, they'd all gathered to mourn the lost dragon. "You miss Sora."

The flurcoons quieted their howl, and they turned their turquoise eyes on Min. They didn't speak words to Min, but she felt their need.

"You knew her?" Min asked.

One of the closest flurcoons made a chittering sound and nodded its head.

"I'll get her back," Min said. "I promise."

"Who are you talking to?"

Min spun toward the new voice, realizing only now that the clearing reeked of human.

Min let her throat fire grow hot. She flapped her wings, arched her neck, and found the source of the sound and smell.

It was a boy. He was younger and shorter than Abigail by four years at least. He had a mess of blond hair, golden brown eyes, and a smattering of freckles across his nose.

He had no sword in his hand or sheathed on his back. He had no weapon at all. He had only a fistful of those strange blue-flower vegetables, fresh dirt still clinging to the roots.

Min showed the boy her teeth. She wasn't here to deal with more humans. She just wanted to find and free Sora and leave.

"You're a dragon!" The boy said, his eyes bright. "Would you like to meet the other dragon?"

Min blinked at the boy. Could he mean Sora? Could this soft little human actually know where Sora was?

"I'll take you to her. It's not too far."

The boy turned and padded back through the grass on bare feet.

Min glanced backward, and the flurcoons—all forty of them—were gone. They must have disappeared down into the ground.

She was alone save the little boy, who was humming an annoying song as he stomped through the meadow.

"The dragon is just through here. I'll show you the way inside."

11

THE BOY TALKED A LOT. He talked about the city of Yawen and how Sora had made it out of the clouds. He talked about how he didn't understand why they could get rain in Yawen when Yawen was a cloud. But they did get rain here, so clouds could rain on other clouds.

And it made the streets smell like flowers. The boy said he thought that was rather odd. He'd heard that when it rained on the land, it also made the air smell like earth and flowers.

"How can that be?"

Min just blinked at the boy. Even if she'd had an answer, which she didn't, the boy wouldn't understand her. He didn't speak Drakon. And she didn't speak Humanish.

The boy turned his round face up to the sky. He squinted, as though it might rain any moment, and the raindrops might splatter him with the answers to his questions.

"I'm Gabe, by the way," he said. "Do you have a name? Sora has a name. But she's a big dragon. And you're very small. Smaller than most birds. Maybe you *are* a bird, not a dragon. I've never seen anything like that before. But I've only ever lived in Yawen. And mostly just in the palace. My mother bakes bread for the nobles. Her bread is the very best in Yawen. She always smells like batches and batches of warm, fresh-baked bread. It's a good smell. But hugging her makes me hungry for bread."

They walked through a tidy garden and entered the tallest tower of Yawen through a back door so tiny it might have been a window. Inside, the air smelled warm and very much like bread.

"Is that you, Gabe?" A woman called from a nearby room. From where they stood, Min could see at least seven doors and a staircase going higher into the tower.

"It's me," Gabe replied, wiping his muddied feet on a mat by the door and dropping the blue-flower vegetables into a hanging basket. "I got two gamja roots."

"Only two?"

"I found a friend. They need help. I'll search for more later."

"Okay, but be back for deliveries."

"I will," Gabe replied, then he motioned for Min to follow.

They hiked the stairs—of course. Min wished Abigail were here with her big, clomping footsteps so that Min could perch on her shoulder and let her human legs do what human legs were supposed to do—walk up stairs.

But Abigail wasn't here. Nor was Kerr, who could have changed the too-tall stairs into a smooth ramp for Min to scurry up.

Min was alone, so she had to climb each stair as if it

were another, tiny peak. Again and again and again.

Min grew tired and, panting hard, curled up to rest on a stair. Gabe tried to pick her up, and she scorched his fingertips with a warning. No one would touch her. No one.

Gabe sucked on a sore finger, tears welling up in his eyes. "I just wanted to help you."

Min stared at the boy. She hadn't burned him much. It was just a little blister of heat. And the boy shouldn't try to touch her. She was a dragon!

A single tear rolled down Gabe's cheek, and Min felt the fire leave her. Her head drooped low, and she felt sad too.

She hadn't really felt bad for hurting a human before. Whether it had been swishing Abigail with her tail or sending the knight, Jurian, falling from his horse, the humans had always deserved the smacking they'd gotten.

And, by all accounts, Gabe had deserved this little burned finger too.

But there was something different about Gabe and his hurt finger. He'd trusted her. He'd never expected her to hurt him. And the tears may very well have more to do with a friend hurting him than with the fire.

"I'm sorry," Min said.

Gabe just blinked another tear down his cheek. He didn't understand Drakon.

Min pushed her tired legs up and under her and walked to Gabe's hand. He flinched away from her, obviously afraid.

But she pressed her forehead to the little burned finger and felt the magic flow through her. She willed the pain away from the boy, and the magic made it happen.

When she opened her eyes and backed away from the boy, his eyes were wide, and a smile spread across his lips.

"I didn't know dragons could do that."

Min let the boy wrap his hands around her body and carry her the rest of the way up the stairs. He wasn't as good at holding her as Abigail was. Abigail respected Min as a dragon and put her on her shoulder or in a satchel. Gabe carried Min under his arm like she was a loaf of bread.

When the boy finally deposited Min on the ground, she had a cramp in her wing and a kink in her neck. But she didn't complain. Gabe wouldn't understand her anyway. And now she knew that the boy was only trying to help.

The room at the top of the stairs was wide and bright, with pillars all around the edges and tall, narrow windows between each pillar showing a bright blue sky.

At the center of the room crouched a massive dragon.

She looked nothing like Kerr. She had a serpentine body with scales that went from dark purple on her tail to a bright turquoise on her head. She had powerful front and back legs with claws as clear as glass. Her belly scales were silver like a stormy sky, and instead of sharp ridges down her back, the dragon had tufts of hair that seemed to move with a wind Min couldn't feel.

"That's our dragon," Gabe said. "That's Sora. I told you I'd bring you to her."

12

MIN WALKED UP TO SORA and felt smaller than she'd ever
felt. The Air Elemental Dragon was three times the size
of Kerr. Min could have fit inside of Sora's nostril, curled
up, and taken a nap there.

"Isn't she beautiful?" Gabe said.

Min nodded. Sora was probably the most beautiful
dragon she'd ever seen. Her scales were colored with a
blend of purple and turquoise. Her folded wings were
elegant. The tufts of fur on her back looked as soft and
wispy as bits of cloud.

Sora was incredible.

Min hurried up to her and stared at Sora's incredible
glass-like claws for a moment. "I am Min," Min said.
"And I am here to free you."

Sora's turquoise eyes twitched down to look at Min.
But the massive dragon didn't move. She didn't speak.
She might as well have been a statue, but for the way her
eyes stared down at Min.

"Wow," Gabe said in a whisper. "I've never seen her do that before."

Min turned to look at Gabe, wishing she'd learned to actually speak a bit of Humanish rather than just understand it.

Gabe must have guessed her confusion. He pointed up at Sora's face. "I've never seen her eyes move. That's incredible!"

"Sora doesn't move?" Min asked.

Gabe shrugged. He didn't understand. But he guessed. "I don't know what you did. But I think she likes you. I've snuck up here every delivery day for years, and I've never seen her move. She doesn't even do that trick for Warlock Rallen, and they've known each other for ages."

Just hearing Warlock Rallen's name made Min want to spit fire. But it also reminded her that the warlock would return soon. And when she did, freeing Sora would be much, much harder.

Min turned back to the enormous dragon, and she realized something wasn't right. It wasn't just that Sora didn't move.

It was that Sora didn't feel like Sora.

This dragon didn't feel like that light, happy, playful, and sad dragon she'd felt somewhere up in the sky. This dragon didn't feel like a dragon at all.

Maybe it was because Sora's mind was gone. Maybe Min had been too late, and now all that was left of Sora had been forgotten.

Min leaned her forehead forward and touched it to the Air Dragon's claw. She held her head there and waited for the magic to tingle up through her body and into Sora.

Nothing happened.

Min raised her head from Sora's foot and twisted her neck to look up at the enormous dragon. "I need you to come with me," Min said. "Let me help you."

Sora stared down at Min. Then her eyes flicked forward and went cold again.

"I won't give up on you," Min said. She rested her head against the Air Dragon's claw once more. She breathed deeply. Maybe she wasn't calm enough. Maybe Sora didn't want to be saved.

No. That was impossible. The ring wanted Min to save Sora next. So here she was. Doing the same thing she'd done to save Kerr.

But it didn't feel right. The magic wasn't coming as it had to heal Gabe's finger and to save Kerr or to heal Abigail's sword wound.

Sora didn't feel right. Why didn't Sora feel right?

"Sora," Min said. "We have to break free of the warlock's control. I have to get you away from here."

The very tip of Sora's tail twitched. Only once.

"You did it AGAIN!" Gabe said. "That's amaz—"

Gabe's voice cut short. And Sora's tail twitched one more time. Her eyes felt angry now, even though they hadn't moved at all.

"What are you doing near my dragon, delivery boy?" A woman somewhere behind them said.

"I-I-I'm so sorry, Warlock Rallen. I was just showing . . . there's another dragon in Yawen. I was introducing her to Sora. I-I-I didn't mean. Please don't kick my mama out of the palace. She makes the very best bread in Ya—"

"Quiet, boy," the woman said.

Min turned slowly from Sora, letting her throat fire build as she did. Warlock Rallen stood beside one of the room's pillars. A long, forest-green cloak hung from the warlock's shoulders, and the hood hid most of the warlock's face in shadow. All except the woman's mouth, which turned into a grim smile. "It's time for me to meet a new dragon," she said in perfect Drakon.

13

MIN CHARGED AT THE WARLOCK, releasing every bit of throat fire she had on Rallen. All of Min's rage at Sora's captivity concentrated into a single burst of flame.

With a flash of purple light, the fire didn't touch the warlock at all. It pushed left and right around her. Rallen laughed. The laugh was high and shrill, like the call of a sick crow.

Min lowered her head, stretched her neck straight, and charged, snapping and biting at the Warlock's legs.

Whatever shield Rallen had made to protect herself from the fire did not work for Min's teeth. The woman danced away from Min's tiny, sharp, angry teeth. But she didn't stop laughing.

Another burst of purple hit Min, and she fell back, sliding across the smooth stone floor toward Sora. Min blinked. The magic sizzled across her scales, and they absorbed much of the attack. The magic that got through made Min's body itch and tingle, but she got to her feet and stood with all her might between Rallen and Sora.

Rallen grinned. Sometime during the commotion, her hood had fallen off, and Min saw the warlock's round face for the first time. Rallen had thick, frizzy red hair with streaks of gray in it and a scar on her chin. She looked amused and mean at the same time, like she used her smile as a weapon. "You are the dragon Tresach spoke of?"

Tresach!

The name made Min angrier still. Tresach was the worst of all the warlocks. He was the enslaver of Orion and the cruel grandfather to Abigail.

If Warlock Rallen had been away from Yawen to speak with Tresach . . .

Then they knew Min would be here. They knew what she was doing. And they'd prepared for her.

Min felt a sinking feeling in her stomach, as though she was falling with her feet still on the ground.

Gabe backed up from Warlock Rallen. His lip was quivering. He looked like he might cry again or run for the door. Instead, he stood beside Min.

"You are trying to protect my dragon?" Rallen laughed, and her eyes glowed a strange purple. "I would never hurt my dragon. You're the one sneaking into Sora's chamber like a thief."

"Let Sora go," Min growled.

Rallen motioned a casual hand up at the dragon. "There are no chains. Sora is as free as you and I."

"You have her magic and her mind," Min breathed the words like fire. "Now give them back."

"We share the magic," Rallen said. "And Sora is entirely content with our arrangement. She stands watch over Yawen, and I maintain the city and help the residents with *our* magic."

"Give. It. Back."

Rallen put her hands on her hips and smiled. "I am not Loatra. Each partnership between dragon and human, each bond, is different. You cannot condemn me for another warlock's wrongs. Loatra is a fool."

Min bared her teeth at the warlock. "You smile and you lie."

"We decide friends and foes," Rallen said, and she extended a hand toward Min. "And I would make you my friend."

Min spat more fire at the warlock. The woman laughed that crow's laugh again.

"There is no one here to save, dragon. Sora is safe. I am nothing like Loatra. You see it with your own eyes."

Min roared at the warlock. She knew the woman was lying. But Rallen was right—Sora didn't look like she was in trouble. And the dragon hadn't followed Min and left before Rallen had returned. Maybe there was more to her prison than Min's eyes could see.

"A feast awaits me," Rallen said. "A celebration of my return. Join me, dragon. And I will prove to you that Sora is well."

Min arched her neck and spat another smattering of flames at Rallen's feet.

"Baker boy," Rallen said.

"Yes?" Gabe replied.

"Would you like to come to my celebration feast?"

Gabe's eyes went wide. "Me?" he asked. "You want me to come?"

"Only if your dragon friend will join you," Rallen said with a tight smile.

Gabe turned on Min in an instant. "Please, red dragon! I've never been to a celebration before! They have cloud dancers. Performing pegasus and all the cakes you can eat!"

Min didn't know many of the words Gabe had just used. She'd never heard of a pegasus. Nor cakes. But the boy looked excited and hopeful.

The idea of it made Min want to roar again. She looked up at Sora and that feeling came back. Something wasn't right, and she needed time to figure it out. She might as well keep the warlock close while she did. "I will go."

14

IT TURNED OUT THAT A PEGASUS was a horse with wings. And cakes were a human food that Gabe could eat so fast it looked like he was breathing them into his stomach. They smelled sweeter than berries. When Min tried a bite, the cake stuck to the top of her mouth. She had to lick and chomp her teeth for ages to get them unglued from each other.

After that, Min did not accept more human food from Gabe. She just sat atop the table and ate a few of the berries piled next to her. Gabe wandered away to try more cakes. Hundreds of humans roamed the room. Eating. Laughing. Smelling terrible.

And all of it made Min miss Abigail. She wished the girl were here to sit beside her, pull out her notebook, and answer Min's questions. Something was wrong with Sora. What Min had done to free Kerr hadn't worked with the Air Dragon. But Abigail would know what to try next.

Sitting in this roomful of humans, who danced

around with puffs of colorful clouds and ate weird food, Min realized that Abigail wasn't as annoying as most humans. Most humans were rather strange. And Min preferred Abigail to all the rest she'd met—although Gabe was mostly tolerable.

Warlock Rallen, on the other hand, was like a sneak beetle.

Sneak beetles looked just like green, crunchy, delicious beetles. Same dark green bodies. Same bright green stripes. They even had the same smell and made the same squeaking sound when Min cornered them.

But a sneak beetle would pretend to be cornered. It would let you get close. Then it would release a burst of foul mist from its mouth—a poison—and the thing would scuttle away.

Min had had a swollen nose for weeks from a sneak beetle.

Warlock Rallen was a sneak beetle.

She acted like the other humans at the feast. She ate and talked and laughed. She watched the dancers and the flying horse. She took bites of the cake—though without the enthusiasm that Gabe had for the sweets.

But something was off about her. Everything she did looked like the humans around her, but it felt wrong. She burned with an intensity that no one else seemed to notice.

She glowed with a magic that wasn't hers.

Rallen looked at Min and smiled. The warlock had a dragon's smile, not a human's. Dragons showed their teeth to challenge another dragon. And Rallen was challenging Min, betting that the little dragon couldn't uncover what was really going on here.

Just then, the flurcoons—five, ten, twenty of them— came out of the floors and walls and ceiling. The little, purple creatures swished their fluffy tails in the air. They scurried with their short legs across the walls and floor. And they destroyed the celebration.

Two flurcoons attacked the cake table, eating and smashing the sweets.

Another flurcoon jumped toward the pegasus.

The flying horse kicked and reared in the air and then charged down to the ground and crashed into a table, turning it into bits and splinters of wood.

People screamed and ran for the doors.

Gabe stood near one of the doors with a piece of cake in one hand and sheer panic on his face as people screamed and charged toward him. The boy looked too surprised to move out of the way, and the fleeing people were more worried about the rampaging flurcoons and horse to see Gabe at all.

Min launched off the table, glided to land in front of Gabe, and flapped her wings wide.

The fleeing humans still didn't notice her, so she released a long jet of flame.

More cries came from the humans, and they dodged around Min and the still too-surprised-to-move Gabe. Min kept shooting fire at the humans' feet until all of them had fled the celebration room. Then she turned to Gabe.

The boy blinked at Min. The room was empty of all humans save him and Rallen. The flurcoons were gnawing on chairs, tugging on tapestries, and ripping torches from the walls. Two of them were covered in cake.

Gabe blinked again. "I'm going home now, red dragon."

Min nodded and Gabe fled after the last humans.

Warlock Rallen sat at the head of a long table, the

flurcoon's destruction happening all around her. Four flurcoons overturned the table. Another three chewed on a painting of Rallen. One flurcoon stomped on the cakes already sprawled across the stone floor. The food made a weird squishing sound beneath the flurcoon's paws.

"That's enough," Rallen said.

The flurcoons hissed at the warlock and continued their tirade.

"ENOUGH!" Rallen shouted. Her eyes glowed purple, and the broken table flickered and returned to normal—all the broken pieces mended in the blink of an eye.

And still the flurcoons attacked. They scratched the tables and walls and floor. They would not stop. Their teeth and claws slashed at everything they could reach.

But why were they so angry?

Min had seen the flurcoons before and played with them in the sky. They hadn't been angry then. They'd been happy and playful and then sad.

They missed Sora. And they weren't just angry. They were angry at *Rallen*.

Warlock Rallen stood, her whole body glowing purple. "You've upset Sora," she said. "Master Tresach ordered me to keep you here. To let Captain Jurian and his knights deal with you." Rallen turned her glowing purple eyes on Min. "But you've upset my dragon. No one upsets my dragon."

15

A TABLE JUST BESIDE MIN EXPLODED in a ball of purple light.

Min shot straight up in the air as high and far as she could get. More purple light whirred past her as she flapped her red wings fast and sure.

The flurcoons launched into the air with Min, ducking and diving around her.

"You cannot save her," Rallen shouted from the ground.

Min turned and wove in the air with the flurcoons. It was like the dance they'd done on the way to the meadow, but this time Warlock Rallen shot bursts of purple magic up at them, trying to blow them out of the sky. But the warlock could only shoot one glowing ball of magic at a time. And the flurcoons flying with Min made too many moving targets.

"Stop it, Sora!" Rallen yelled.

Min turned her head, looking around for the Air

Dragon. But all she saw were flurcoons.

Rallen threw magic at them faster and faster. Walls exploded. Windows shattered. The ceiling above them creaked, and dust fell on them all like rain.

The flurcoons pulled Min out one of the broken walls and into the sky. As soon as they'd exited the tower, Min felt a rush of relief. She'd survived Warlock Rallen!

From the height of the tower, Min could see the whole city of Yawen. The flurcoons still pulled her along, but she marveled at the beauty of the city and wondered how a warlock as twisted and ugly inside as Rallen could have helped make this place.

That's when Min spotted the little black flecks in the clouds on the far side of the city. They looked like black leaves spinning in the wind. Min's relief and excitement at surviving Rallen faded to fear.

The dorcha were coming.

And, as they came closer, Min could spot humans in shiny armor perched on the creatures' backs.

Rallen had said that Tresach's knights would come to deal with Min. Here they were, riding on the backs of the dorcha.

16

ABIGAIL WALKED SIDE BY SIDE WITH KERR through a village as if it were the most normal thing in all the world to walk with a dragon down a street.

In most of Golshan, dragons were a rarity. Only a few of the biggest cities had a dragon at all. And, even then, the dragon wasn't usually wandering down city streets or taking a nap on a hillside.

No, most people would count themselves lucky just to see a dragon.

And here Abigail was walking and talking to one, learning about magic and the history of the world from one of the dragons that actually created it!

The village they passed through had three roads and ten buildings. All of it rested at the top of a breezy hill where rocks seemed to grow instead of grass. Purple flags waved from a single wooden post that stuck up over the housetops.

The sky train would arrive there. According to

Abigail's research, Sora's power reached down in an invisible rope from Yawen to that pole. The sky train—a big metal box—moved up and down the invisible rope, taking people and supplies to and from the city in the sky.

"Was the sky train Sora's idea?" Abigail asked as they passed the second street. They were almost to the pole and the sky train station now.

"Yes," Kerr said. "Sora had been so pleased with Yawen, she'd wanted everyone to visit it. Well, everyone except me. I admired it from a safe distance."

"Why do Air and Earth magic react to each other?" Abigail asked.

"Why does water extinguish fire?" Kerr replied. "Magic is an extension of the natural order. There must be balance. Even among the dragons."

Abigail pulled out her notebook and quill from her satchel and began writing. "If every dragon has an element that they're weak against, what are you weak against?"

"Ice," Kerr said with a little shiver.

"Fascinating!" Abigail exclaimed and made another note.

Kerr stopped short and stared up at the sky. Abigail paused her writing and stared at the dragon. At first she thought she'd offended Kerr by asking him about his elemental weakness. She opened her mouth to begin an apology, but Kerr spoke first.

"Min's in trouble."

Abigial squinted up at the sky. She couldn't see anything different in the clouds. "What do you see?"

"I feel it," Kerr said. "We need to get you to Yawen. Fast."

Abigial slammed her notebook shut and ran toward the sky train station. Kerr loped with heavy footsteps beside her. She arrived at the pole a breathless moment later. A wooden staircase circled the pole and led to a wooden platform where the sky train would arrive. But no sky train was there now.

Abigail read the signs posted to the pole and found the schedule. "The next train comes at high noon."

They both glanced at the sun. That was at least an hour's wait. Maybe more.

"Min can't wait that long," Kerr said. "Get on my back."

Abigail blinked at the dragon. "You can't fly to Yawen."

"I'm not flying to Yawen. I'm taking you to a sky train that's on its way to Yawen," Kerr said. "Now get on."

"What can I do?" Abigail asked, holding her notebook to her chest and feeling her heartbeat pounding hard against it. "I'm not a dragon. I'm not a warlock, yet. I-I'm just a girl."

"You're Min's friend," Kerr said. "And she needs one now."

With her notebook tucked under her arm, Abigail scrambled up Kerr's leg and shoulder and then hesitated there.

Kerr lurched into the air, and Abigail almost tumbled off. Then she hurriedly sat down, clung to one of Kerr's back spikes with one arm, and carried her notebook in the other. "We're coming Min," Abigail said under her breath as the wind roared around her. "We're coming."

17

THE FLURCOONS GUIDED MIN back to the meadow, and Min landed in the swaying golden grass. Her heart beat fast.

She'd barely survived one battle against Rallen, and now a squad of knights was almost upon her. She likely wouldn't survive another fight—not alone.

The flurcoons, bouncing and running in the same direction, disappeared into the grass. Purple fluffs of color swallowed by the yellow meadow.

Min followed the flurcoons. She wasn't sure why she was following them. She should probably head back into the tower and try to free Sora again. With the Air Dragon's help, she could face down Rallen and a full squad of knights.

But she followed the flurcoons instead. Her feet had a mind of their own, and the rest of her was not quite sure what to do.

She stopped at the clearing—the one big enough for

three Kerr's to land—at the center of the meadow. The flurcoons sat around the border of the clearing. Each of the rambunctious creatures was unnaturally calm.

One of the flurcoons moved from the line and stood in front of Min. It stared deep into Min's eyes, as if it were trying to yell an answer at her with just one look.

Then the flurcoon twitched the end of its tail.

Min gasped.

"You're Sora!"

The flurcoon's tail flicked faster, but Min didn't need the flurcoon to speak. That feeling she'd had back at camp matched everything she'd felt from the flurcoons—playful and happy as she'd flown in the air with them. And sad and quiet in this very grass.

Min didn't know how it was possible, but these flurcoons were really Sora.

Now that she knew it in her heart, the way Rallen yelled at the flurcoons made more sense. She'd called them Sora.

But how could Sora be these flurcoons and also the dragon up in the tower?

"It must be an illusion!" Min shouted "A trick Rallen used when Sora turned into the flurcoons! The people love Sora. They wouldn't like Sora to be gone."

The flurcoon, tail flicking and eyes eager, just waited for Min.

Min took a deep breath and steadied her mind. "I see you, Sora," Min said, and she touched her forehead to the flurcoon's head. "I am here to help you."

Min closed her eyes and felt the magic tickling through her body.

18

THE FLURCOONS WERE SORA!

Min felt that jolt of magic when she pressed her forehead to the flurcoon, just as she had when she'd found Kerr in the caverns beneath the city of Avani.

She had found Sora, but that didn't mean she'd saved her. Not yet.

Min opened her eyes, but she wasn't in Yawen anymore. She wasn't sitting in the swaying golden grass with her head pressed against a flurcoon's head.

She was in Sora's mind.

Clouds encircled them. The sun crested through the clouds, turning them into brushes of red and purple across the sky.

A single flurcoon with turquoise eyes flew nearby. It paused when it saw Min and cocked its head to stare at her.

"What are you?" it asked.

"I am Min. I am a dragon."

"A dragon?" The flurcoon flicked its tail. "I like dragons."

"You are a dragon, Sora."

"Me?" The creature laughed. Her voice was light as air. "I am a flurcoon."

"You're not," Min said. "You're a dragon."

"I look like a flurcoon," the animal said, twisting around and hugging her fluffy, purple tail. "I feel like a flurcoon."

"You're a dragon," Min said. "You made Yawen. You helped make this world!"

The flurcoon spun in the air, seeming to float without any effort at all, while Min flapped her wings hard to keep steady. "I fly like a flurcoon," she said.

"But you're a dragon. You have to listen to me!"

"I could listen to you," the flurcoon said. "Or I could leave." The creature flicked its tail and dove into a pile of clouds.

"No! Sora!" Min flapped her wings and chased the streak of purple through the brilliant landscape of clouds and sunrise.

Min sped through the clouds, pushing her wings faster and faster. The flurcoon dove lower and lower and lower, breaking through each layer of clouds below them. Min followed, bursting through one after another after another until she broke through the last of the clouds and found . . .

There was no ground.

Below her, where there should be a distant glimpse of the ocean or mountains or grassland or desert, there was just more and more sky.

There was nowhere to land—nowhere to rest. Min was trapped in a world of clouds and air, and all she could think about was falling.

Her stomach churned and twisted. Her head got dizzy, and all the clouds and color blended into a blur. She kept flapping her wings, but they grew heavier and heavier with each second.

She was going to fall.

Even as she thought about falling, it began to happen. She fell backwards. The wind pressed in all around her as she fell faster and faster. She thought about the fight with the murada lizard and the way her wing had stopped working. She hadn't been able to stop the fall no matter how she'd tried.

Falling is part of flying, Little One.

Kerr's words echoed in her mind, as though he were flying beside her now. She felt his mind close. His voice close.

She closed her eyes, tucked her wings in close to her body, and let herself fall. She relaxed into the sensation and felt the wind pressing against her scales. It gave her wings a rest from their work.

And the fear beating hard in her mind and body went quiet.

The fear was still there. She still didn't want to crash into the ground and get hurt. But she could control the fear. She could make it quiet.

Min opened her eyes and found the flurcoon diving through the sky beside her. Her turquoise eyes were curious and sad and staring right at Min.

Min opened her wings up and turned fast. She flapped away from the flurcoon, giving the other dragon something to chase.

Dragons were hunters. Like Min on the beach with the crabs. Maybe, if Min could remind Sora of that, Min could remind her of more.

A laugh boomed behind Min, and it wasn't the

chittering sound of a flurcoon. It was a dragon's voice—deep and powerful and happy.

Min led Sora on a twisting, turning, looping chase through purple clouds and blue sky and bouts of misty rain. After the mighty chase was done, Sora caught Min.

But it wasn't a flurcoon that had Min in its grip. It was a massive purple and turquoise foot with glass-like claws. Sora had transformed back into a dragon!

She held Min gently and flew toward the sun. Sora flew faster than Min had ever flown, faster than she'd ever imagined anything could fly.

"I am a dragon!" Sora roared, and she bent the clouds around her. She shaped them with her mind into towers, then humans, then dragons, then chains that burst into pieces.

"You are a dragon!" Min yelled up at Sora. "And you are free!"

19

MIN OPENED HER EYES, and she was back in the meadow with the golden grass. The flurcoons were climbing on top of each other, making a giant pile of wiggling, chittering creatures. When all the flurcoons were in the pile, they glowed purple. The light was so bright, Min had to look away.

When she could see again, Sora the dragon was standing where the flurcoons had been.

This Sora was even more majestic and beautiful than the illusion in the tower or the Sora in her mind. She was long and lean with tufts of hair all along her back. Her belly scales were the brightest silver, and the rest of her shifted from purple on her tail to turquoise by her nose. She looked down at Min with joy in her eyes.

And that was the most beautiful thing of all.

Min moved closer and closer to Sora's face like she was flying upward, but she wasn't flapping her wings. She wasn't moving at all.

Then Min felt that tingling of magic in her body, tickling her from head to tail and from wing to wing. Min was transforming too!

When the magic was done, Min stood as tall as Sora's shoulder, and she was high enough to see over every building in Yawen. Her body was the same long, elegant shape, and her colors matched the purple, turquoise, and silver of Sora. Min even had small fluffs of hair down her spine.

"You look like me," Sora said.

"Yes," Min said. "It's part of what Orion's ring does. When I free you, I transform into a dragon that looks like you. But only for a little while."

"I dreamt of you," she said, and her voice was a gentle breeze. "But I kept forgetting. I . . . it was hard to think of anything. But I knew I'd dreamt of you."

"Rallen made you forget," Min said. "She wanted your mind so she could have your power."

Sora growled, and the sound was low and dangerous. "She will know the fury of the skies when I find her."

Min looked about the city and spotted the dorcha and their knights landing at the edges of Yawen.

Sora clacked her teeth together in a challenge. "Who dares invade my city?"

"Rallen brought them," Min said. "I think they're Tresach's knights come to take me away."

"They will not harm you. Or my city," Sora said.

"It might be a trap," Min said, "to lure us over there. Rallen is smart. If she didn't follow me here, she has another plan."

Sora growled again, and the sound shook the air.

"Rallen knew I was here to free you. She's going to expect you to go and fight," Min said.

"And I will go."

"Rallen will be prepared for you," Min said. "But she won't be prepared for me."

"What are you planning?"

"You made the flurcoons before, when your mind was lost," Min said, a smile growing on her face. "Could you make them again?"

"I can," Sora said.

"Then we will meet Tresach's army with our own," Min said.

20

KERR FLEW THROUGH THE SKY with Abigail clinging to his back.

It was very cold flying on the back of a dragon. Her fingers were frozen from the cold air, and she barely kept her grip on her notebook and Kerr's spike.

A sky train slid sideways through the air in front of them. If Abigail hadn't been riding on a dragon, she would have thought the bit of magical engineering was moving quite quickly. But Kerr caught up to the flying metal rectangle easily.

Kerr came upon the sky train silently and swiftly, like an owl ambushing a mouse. And Abigail wondered just how terrifying it would be to make an enemy of a dragon.

Kerr hovered above the sky train and then landed on the house-sized box. He gripped it with his front and back claws and flapped his wings to keep most of his weight off the box.

"Go, Abigail," Kerr said.

Abigail's legs were numb from the cold wind. But she leaned forward, wiggled her wobbly legs beneath her, and half-climbed, half-fell off Kerr's back.

Once she was on the top of the sky train, she knelt and grabbed hold of some cargo ropes. It might have been an exhilarating feeling, riding atop that sky train, if she hadn't just been riding on the back of a dragon.

Kerr let go of the sky train. "Help Min. I will watch for my chance to do the same."

"Be safe, Kerr," Abigail called out as Kerr turned to fly away.

The Earth Dragon laughed, and the happy rumble filled Abigail with comfort.

"We are more than our fears," Kerr said, and he pivoted in the air.

Abigail clutched the cargo ropes with her numb fingers. "Today, we have to be."

21

A SKY TRAIN slid sideways through the air in front of them. If Abigail hadn't been riding on a dragon, she would have thought the bit of magical engineering was moving quite quickly. But Kerr caught up to the flying metal rectangle easily.

Kerr came upon the sky train silently and swiftly, like an owl ambushing a mouse. And Abigail wondered just how terrifying it would be to make an enemy of a dragon.

Kerr hovered above the sky train and then landed on the house-sized box. He gripped it with his front and back claws and flapped his wings to keep most of his weight off the box.

"Go, Abigail," Kerr said.

Abigail's legs were numb from the cold wind. But she leaned forward, wiggled her wobbly legs beneath her, and half-climbed, half-fell off Kerr's back.

Once she was on the top of the sky train, she knelt

and grabbed hold of some cargo ropes. It might have been an exhilarating feeling, riding atop that sky train, if she hadn't just been riding on the back of a dragon.

Kerr let go of the sky train. "Help Min. I will watch for my chance to do the same."

"Be safe, Kerr," Abigail called out as Kerr turned to fly away.

The Earth Dragon laughed, and the happy rumble filled Abigail with comfort.

"We are more than our fears," Kerr said, and he pivoted in the air.

Abigail clutched the cargo ropes with her numb fingers. "Today, we have to be."

22

MIN WALKED THROUGH YAWEN and toward Tresach's knights. People stopped and gawked at her, calling her Sora.

They didn't know better. Aside from a smaller stature and the golden ring on her neck, she looked very much like the Air Dragon.

Which was exactly the plan.

Warlock Rallen was a sneak beetle. She wasn't going to come out and face them without the knights at her side. She'd laid this trap for the dragons to walk into.

But she'd expected Sora and a small red dragon.

Now, Sora seemed to walk right up to the trap, but the real Sora had taken to the skies. And she'd have her own surprise for Rallen and the knights.

But right now, Min had to face down Rallen and the knights by herself, if only for a little while.

Min's heart thundered in her chest. It sounded loud in

her ears. She couldn't decide if it was because she was doing something incredibly dangerous or because she was bigger now and her heart sounds were bigger too.

She crossed the last bridge to where the sky trains docked and a flock of dorcha sat perched. The giant bats screeched at Min, pulling at the ropes that kept them there. Thirty knights, weapons bared, stood at the ready in front of the dorcha. They didn't seem to notice the dorcha growing more and more agitated as Min—wearing Orion's ring on her neck—approached.

The knight called Jurian and Master Rallen were at the head of the formation. Jurian was the only knight without his sword and shield drawn. Rallen stood with her deep green cloak and red hair billowing in the wind. Her hands glowed with stolen purple magic, and a cruel smile twisted her lips.

"Return to my control, Sora," Rallen shouted up at Min. "And I will not harm you."

Min wanted to laugh, but she kept her face solemn. Rallen hadn't recognized the younger, smaller version of Sora as different. She didn't know it was Min. And they didn't want to attack Sora. Not when her magic kept the city of Yawen up in the sky. If they harmed her, the whole city could fall to the ground.

But fooling the warlock was only the first part of the plan. The second was to get her to use her magic. Min lowered her head a little closer to Rallen and Jurian. She opened her mouth as though to speak . . .

And roared at them instead.

Everything inside her wanted to blow out fire too. But she couldn't use her own power. She needed the warlock to use magic first.

Jurian staggered backward. Several of the knights fell over. All of them covered their ears and shouted. And a little boy cried out in terror—a boy she recognized in an instant.

"Gabe!" Min yelled.

Gabe had been hidden among the knights. Now Jurian grabbed the young boy by the wrist and hauled him forward. Then he drew his sword and held the blade to Gabe's neck.

23

"DON'T YOU TOUCH HIM!" Min roared.

Rallen struck out with an orb of purple magic. The magic exploded across Min's chest. Her scales lessened some of the spell's power, but it still burned and itched and burned some more. She wanted to spit fire at the knights and to chase Jurian away from Gabe. But she couldn't use her magic. Not right now. Not right here.

Because the dorcha needed to focus on a new enemy.

The bat-like creatures lurched from their perches, broke the ropes that kept them there, and attacked Warlock Rallen from all sides.

The warlock screamed and shot more and more magic at them, but the magic only made the dorcha angrier.

Kerr had told Min that the dorcha despised magic—Warlock magic most of all.

Surely the knights had decided to use the dorcha

because the creatures disliked magic and would hunt through the clouds after dragons. But they hadn't guessed the giant bats would turn on the warlock. Some of the knights tried to stop the dorcha and save Rallen, but most of them turned their weapons toward Min.

Min's throat fire grew hotter and hotter. In her Air Dragon form, she could melt all of these knights' armor in an instant.

Jurian tightened his grip on Gabe. "Get back, dragon," he said in Humanish. "I know you're the little red one. I see the ring on your neck."

Gabe made a whimpering sound. He had a satchel of bread clutched to his chest. He'd probably been out making deliveries when Rallen had found him. She must have known Min would protect the boy again and had snatched him so she could control at least one of the dragons coming to her trap. But Rallen hadn't known Min was going to be in the form of the Air Dragon.

Jurian, however, knew it was Min as soon as he'd seen the ring on her neck. He'd seen her before during the fight to save Abigail after rescuing Kerr. He'd tried to kill her after she'd become small again.

And now he pressed the sword closer to Gabe's neck. "Give me the ring, red dragon, and I won't hurt this boy."

Min bared her teeth at the knight. If she gave the ring to Jurian, he'd take it back to Tresach, and Min wouldn't be able to save any more dragons. Orion's plan would fail. There would be no more Dragon Champion.

But if she didn't give the ring to Jurian, then Gabe would get hurt for being Min's friend.

"You understand me," Jurian said. He didn't smile. He didn't seem to like having the sword to the boy's throat. "I don't want to hurt him. I just need the ring."

Min felt that familiar tingling down her spine and

across her wings. The magic that made her large would soon leave her, and she'd go back to being small.

Small enough the knight could just capture Min and wrestle the ring off her neck with force.

She didn't have much time.

A tear ran down Gabe's cheek. "Please, Sora. Help me."

Min sighed, and her breath was hot with the fire she couldn't let out. Then she lowered her head toward the knight and showed him her neck and the ring there. "Take it," she said.

Jurian eyed her. He didn't speak Drakon, but he knew she could have blown fire at him instead.

"Get the ring!" He yelled at the knights around him. Several moved away from Rallen or got up from the ground to hurry toward Min.

They put their hands on Min's neck, on the ring. And Min just looked into Gabe's terrified face, wishing the boy could understand her. Wishing she could tell him it was going to be okay.

24

ABIGAIL HID BEHIND AN EMPTY SKY TRAIN watching the chaos unfold.

When the sky train she'd been riding had landed in Yawen, she'd expected some city officials—or maybe even Warlock Rallen herself—to surround the sky train, demand that Abigail get off the roof, and take her right to their dungeon.

But as soon as Abigail arrived, so did a flock of dorcha with Tresach's own knights seated on their backs.

That was enough to distract everyone on the docking platform, so Abigail was able to climb off the metal box, slip into the crowd of confused traders, and then dart out of the crowd to hide behind an empty sky train.

She watched there for a few moments. Her heart beat fast when she saw Warlock Rallen meet Jurian and his knights. They'd clearly planned the meeting, and they only spoke for a few minutes. The warlock had a young boy by the wrist, and she handed him over to Jurian.

Jurian didn't take the boy at first. He argued with the warlock, and her eyes shone purple. A threat of magic. Only then did the knight grab the boy and then take up position with his knights facing the city. Waiting.

An air dragon approached only moments later. Abigail thought the air dragon was Sora. Then she spotted the golden ring on the dragon's neck. She wanted to run out to her friend, but she kept to the shadows. Min just walked into the ambush, but Abigail needed to find the right moment to help. She didn't want to become another hostage for Jurian and his knights.

Min roared at Warlock Rallen. Jurian threatened the boy. And Rallen attacked Min with magic.

And the magic drove the dorcha mad.

They burst from their tethers and ambushed the warlock.

Abigail grinned. Min had listened! She'd learned from Abigail and Kerr and had used cleverness, not just strength, to battle the warlock.

With two enemies distracted, Min should be able to dispatch Jurian and his knights and escape. But Min didn't move. She didn't attack.

Instead, she lowered her head near Jurian and let the knights rush toward her. And they began to pull Orion's ring off her neck!

Abigail couldn't believe her eyes. Why would Min allow *anyone* to touch Orion's ring? Why wouldn't she fight the knights? She'd be eager, in her Air Dragon form, to show them just how fierce a dragon could be!

Then Abigail saw the boy again. He was probably close to ten years old with a mess of blond hair and a satchel clutched to his chest.

Jurian had his sword pressed to the boy's throat. That's why Min wasn't attacking. That's why she was letting the knights try to pull the ring from her neck.

Abigail ran from her hiding place with no plan, but an anger in her belly as fierce as any dragon's fire. She kept to the edges of the dock. The dorcha swooped down and screeched and clawed at Warlock Rallen. The warlock hit them with orbs of purple magic, and one by one they fell to the ground dead.

In the chaos of the battle, Jurian didn't notice Abigail running at him. His eyes were forward, watching his knights wrestle the ring a little farther off Min's neck. Jurian smiled, and the boy in his hands made a little whimpering sound.

Mere feet from Jurian, Abigail realized she had no weapon. All she had was her beloved notebook that was always in her hands. She ran up on the captain of the knights and clobbered him in the back of the head with her heavy notebook.

Jurian made a gasping sound and turned toward Abigail, releasing the boy.

Abigail hit him again, and he crumpled to the ground with a clang of armor. The boy ran at Abigail and wrapped his arms around her waist, burying his face in her and crying. Abigail held him in her arms and met Min's eyes. "Get them," Abigail said in Drakon.

25

MIN ATTACKED.

She shook their hands free from her neck and Orion's ring, and she let out her throat fire in a terrific roar. The knights fell back. Their hair lit on fire. Their armor became scalding hot. They fled from her, and their captain was still unconscious on the ground.

Min took one step toward Abigail and Gabe when a purple light exploded across her back. She roared in pain. The purple magic stole Min's strength, and her legs gave out beneath her. She fell to the ground. Her heart beat fast and her throat fire grew cold in her chest. Warlock Rallen strode to Min, stopping in front of her eyes.

"Master Tresach warned me about you," Rallen said with a laugh. "He doesn't waste words. But I still didn't believe a little dragon could do all of this."

Min bared her teeth. She tried to summon her fire, but her insides felt as cold as ice. She didn't hear any dorcha—Rallen must have defeated them all. Without any other targets to distract the warlock, Rallen had used all of her power in one devastating blow against Min.

Rallen was stronger than Min had thought.

"You may have Orion's ring," Rallen said, "but you know nothing about magic."

The warlock clapped her hands together and then slowly pulled them apart. A ball of purple magic grew in the space between her fingers. In moments her hands were spread wide, and a crackling orb of magic, bigger than any Rallen had yet made, floated above her head.

"I will take you and the girl back to Master Tresach," Rallen said. "He doesn't really care if you are alive or dead when I take you to him."

"No!" Abigail shouted. She pushed Gabe behind her and glared at Rallen. "You won't take us anywhere."

Rallen laughed. "Are you going to stop me? You have had this dragon with you for weeks now, but you still haven't bonded with it. You have no power to stop me, apprentice."

Rallen turned back to Min, and she raised her hands even higher in the air. All she had to do was bring her arms back down, and she'd drop the magical attack on Min.

Min's tail and wings and neck tickled with a different kind of magic. She smiled weakly up at Rallen. "I'm ready, Warlock. Do your worst."

Rallen sneered and threw the purple ball of magic at Min.

In an instant, Min's body was overcome by the tickling magic, and she transformed back into her small, red self. She wasn't sure how she knew she could change her body from big to small on purpose. She just knew. That's how Dragon magic worked sometimes; she just got the idea that she could do something and then she could do it.

The magic ball flew far over Min's head. It collided with a sky train and knocked the thing off the platform, sending it crashing through the clouds below.

Rallen screamed her frustration into the sky.

And a dragon's roar came as a reply. But it wasn't Min who made the sky shake with the sound.

It was Sora.

26

THE AIR DRAGON FLEW DOWN FROM THE CLOUDS. But Sora wasn't alone. Thousands and thousands of purple fluffs dove and spun and twirled with her.

Sora had made a flurcoon army, and they were coming for Rallen.

Rallen cursed the Air Dragon and summoned a smaller ball of purple magic. She threw the ball at Sora, but a flurcoon caught it instead.

Rallen threw more and more magic up at Sora, but each time a flurcoon would catch the magic and hold it.

Sora landed in front of Rallen. Her massive body barely fit on the platform. Min rallied her strength and got to her feet. She swayed a little, her head dizzy, but she walked to stand beside Sora's front foot.

"Are you okay, Little Red?" Sora asked.

"This wasn't my best plan," Min replied, "but I'm okay."

"Sora," Rallen said, her voice shaking. The warlock

sounded afraid. Her face looked afraid. But something wasn't right with this sneak beetle.

Rallen took a few steps backward toward the edge of the platform. "I-I didn't mean to . . ."

"You will return my magic now," Sora said. "Our bond is over."

Rallen crept backward again. "I just wanted to-to . . ."

"I will not listen to your lies. Your time with magic is done," Sora said.

Rallen stopped. She now stood at the edge of the platform. But she didn't look afraid anymore. She looked happy. Why did she look happy?

The sneak beetle was trying to escape!

"Stop her!" Min shouted.

Rallen smiled, turned, and jumped off the platform.

"No!" Abigail and Min shouted at once.

Sora cocked her head. "Why do we care if she falls?"

"She still has your magic," Min said, running on her short legs to the edge of the platform. "We need her to return it to you."

Rallen fell through the clouds, using bursts of purple magic to move left and right. She might even be able to make it to the ground without dying.

Sora and Min both lowered their bodies closer to the ground, preparing to leap off the platform. But before they could jump, a mass of green and gold spun through the air and snatched the warlock in its claws.

"Kerr!" Min shouted.

27

THE EARTH DRAGON ROARED A GREETING and threw the warlock up in the air. Rallen screamed as she suddenly went from falling to being thrown back toward Yawen.

Sora flicked her head, and flurcoons caught the warlock and brought her to the platform. They held down her legs and arms so she couldn't move.

"You cannot take my power," Rallen hissed. "It's mine! You gave it to me! It's mine!"

"I trusted you," Sora said. "We were friends, and I gave you all."

Rallen glared at both dragons. "You should have let me fall."

Min walked to Rallen. Her legs were still weak from Rallen's attack, but she made the distance without falling over. When she was close, she reached one foot out and touched it to Rallen's boot.

The warlock screamed and tried to kick and thrash Min away, but the flurcoons held her steady. As soon as

Min touched Rallen, she felt Sora's magic leap into her own body. The dragon's magic wanted to return to a dragon. It wanted to return to Sora. Min roared and the sound wasn't her own. It shattered the sky and brought a light rain trickling down on them all.

"No," Rallen whispered, but the deed was done. The magic, Sora's magic, was gone and Rallen was a warlock no more.

Min walked back to Sora, and the Air Dragon lowered her head to the ground. Even so, Min could only press her forehead to Sora's chin. "This is yours," Min said.

The magic fled Min and entered Sora once more. Sora sighed and then roared again. The sound was joyful. It brought more rain in bigger and bigger drops, cleansing Yawen and bringing the smell of earth and flowers to the air.

28

It took twenty minutes to convince Gabe to get near Sora. The boy kept shaking his head and saying that this wasn't Sora. Sora didn't move. The real dragon was up in the tower. This dragon was something different.

"That's Sora!" Min said, but the boy didn't understand Drakon, so Abigail had to translate.

Fortunately, Abigail was more patient than Min. She knelt beside the boy and gave him a gentle smile. "It seems impossible to be this close to an Elemental Dragon, doesn't it?"

The boy looked up at Sora with wide eyes. "She moves so much. Why does she move so much?"

"You're used to an illusion of a dragon," Abigail said. "The real Sora is as alive as you and me. And right now we would like to introduce her to the rest of Yawen. Would you like to help us?"

"Is she going to hurt us?"

Abigail laughed. "Sora made Yawen. She loves the

people here."

Gabe worked on that bit of information for a moment, and he gathered some of his courage. "Could we introduce her to my mother? My mother's never seen Sora. Not even the fake one."

Abigail's smile grew wider. "Yes. Let's go introduce Sora to all of Yawen and your mother."

Gabe smiled a little too. "Can I lead the way?"

Abigail looked up at Sora, and the big dragon rumbled a laugh. "Yes," Sora said. "He may lead."

Abigail told Gabe the news, and he looked excitedly up at Sora and then back to Min. "I think I'm going to like the new Sora," he said.

***

They walked through Yawen with Gabe in front, Min and Abigail behind him, and Sora at the back.

The people of Yawen crept out of their houses to stare at the dragon. And every time they did, Abigail explained that Warlock Rallen had betrayed her city and her dragon, but Sora was back.

A cheer rose around them, and the people began to spread the news on their own. Soon the whole city seemed to be celebrating their dragon.

Sora bowed before a group of cheering citizens. Gabe cheered along with them, and Min and Abigail stood a ways off watching the celebration.

"Sora is happy to be done with her bond," Abigail said.

"Sora is happy to be a dragon again," Min said.

Abigail looked down at Min. "Do you think a dragon and a human can bond and be happy?"

"Yes," Min said. And she said the word with conviction. Abigail smiled at Min.

Min smiled back. "Well, as long as the human doesn't

smell too bad. And she carries her dragon when the dragon's legs are tired."

Abigail raised an eyebrow at Min. "Are your legs tired?"

Min shrugged. "Maybe. But we're not bonded. So I'll have to walk."

Abigail laughed and scooped up Min gently in her hands. "Bonded or not, we're still friends."

Min melted a little in the warmth and careful attention of her friend's embrace. She closed her eyes. "Friends feed each other bread too."

Abigail laughed again. "They do?"

"Not just any bread. The bread Gabe's mom makes. It's the best in Yawen."

"You want me to feed you bread?" Abigail asked.

"Maybe," Min said with a smile. Just happy that her friend was near.

29

THE NEXT DAY, Min found herself back at the sky train platform. This time she was waiting for Abigail. All of the knights had been rounded up and put in the Yawen jail. All except for their captain, Jurian, who had escaped when Rallen jumped from the platform. They didn't think he'd left the city, but the citizens of Yawen were searching for him now.

Min looked back at the city and its tower.

"Yawen is so beautiful," Min said. The buildings made of clouds took on the light of the new sunrise, absorbing the reds and purples and golds. The city glowed with new hope.

"I am starting to remember the time before." Sora scooped Min up with a careful paw and dropped the little red dragon on top of her head. Sitting on the forehead of Sora the Air Dragon, Min felt smaller than she ever had before. But at this height, Min could see all of Yawen and miles and miles of clouds beyond.

"I remember what Rallen was like when I first met her. When we first bonded," Sora said. "We used to watch the sunrises together. We used to talk about a city we could make in the sky. About the dreamers that would follow us there. This was our greatest work, and she turned it into a prison. But not all humans are like Rallen."

Min stretched her wings, and her belly still felt round and full from eating so much of Gabe's mother's bread. "Yeah. Some humans make yummy bread."

"Abigail isn't like other humans," Sora said.

"I know," Min replied.

"You two will create wonderful things together. Greater than Rallen and I ever did."

Min sat down on the big dragon's head. "Maybe. But freeing you is good enough for me."

"That is a good start," Sora said with a laugh. "Thank you, Min. Thank you for finding me. For seeing me and saving me."

"I only did it for the bread," Min said, and Sora laughed again. Min smiled a human smile.

Abigail hurried onto the platform, and her arms were full of books. "Rallen had a library," she said.

"How will you carry all of those books around all the time?" Min asked.

Abigail shrugged and almost dropped all of the books. "I'll have to read them one at a time."

"Now that I want to see," Min said.

Abigail smiled, then looked toward the sky train. "I'll take the sky train down and meet you on the ground."

"No," Sora said. "I will take you to the ground."

Abigail bounced with excitement and almost dropped the pile of books again. "You will? Thank you!"

Min stood up and stretched her wings. The wind

pressed against her red scales, and she loved the feel of it. "I'll race you down," Min said.

And without waiting for Sora to reply, Min dove off the enormous dragon's nose and into the clouds, dipping and twirling, diving and soaring—feeling the fear of falling and the joy of flying all at once.

END OF BOOK TWO

Becca Lee Gardner

Author's Letter

I was afraid to write Min the Fearless.

I know, it's funny that I was afraid to write a book that I later named "fearless," but that's the truth.

You see, I wrote Min the Mighty when no one was looking. It had been a bedtime story I told my kiddos. I later wrote it into a book on a whim and hid it away. Liam and Todd championed it into publication in 2022.

Since then, I've met countless fans of the book. I've talked with them at markets and at schools. I've seen the excitement in their eyes.

People were watching this series. They were excited for the next book. And, oddly enough, that terrified me.

I didn't know how to start this book. I wasn't sure where Min should grow and what she should learn. So I used the fear I was feeling and made that the place where Min began.

Thank you all for caring so deeply about Min and the Elemental Dragons she's here to save. I write every day (afraid or no) for each of you.

-BECCA

ALSO BY BECCA LEE GARDNER

Eldros Legacy
Worldbreaker: An Eldros Legacy Novel

The Storm Chronicles
Mindstorm

Dragon Champion Series
Min the Mighty
Min the Fearless
Min the Protector
Min the Valiant
Min the Relentless
Min the Undaunted
Min the Champion

The Hybrid World
The Forest Glows

Short Stories
Delilah's Valor
Yellow Monroe
Confession
Imani
The Human Pet Called Grek
The Yeti Mystic
The Valkyries Initiative: *Surprise*
Of Wizards and Wolves A Dave Farland Memorial Anthology:
The Punstoppable Catfish Stanley

ABOUT THE AUTHOR

Becca Lee Gardner is an 8-time Honorable Mention Winner from the Writers of the Future contest. She writes novels, comic books, screenplays, and short stories. Her sci-fi horror novella, *Mindstorm*, debuted in December of 2021. If it's science fiction or fantasy with monsters in it, she's all in.

When she's not writing, Becca walks for hours and hours, chasing the sunrise. She also plays intense rounds of Marvel Splendor and Star Wars: Battlefront with her three kids. Her favorite evenings are spent watching Korean zombie shows with her husband who jump-scares quite easily.

Connect with Becca on Facebook: https://www.facebook.com/beccaleeg

And Instagram: https://www.instagram.com/beccaleeg/

Or via email at beccaleegardner@gmail.com.

(Photo cred: Norma Carver)